Get set with Read Alone!

This entertaining series is designed for all new readers who want to start reading a whole book on their own.

The stories are lively and fun, with lots of illustrations and clear, large type, to make first solo reading a perfect pleasure!

Willie Whiskers

Margaret Gordon

VIKING KESTREL

VIKING KESTREL

Published by the Penguin Group
27 Wrights Lane, London W8 5TZ, England
Viking Penguin Inc., 40 West 23rd Street, New York, New York 10010, USA
Penguin Books Australia Ltd, Ringwood, Victoria, Australia
Penguin Books Canada Ltd, 2801 John Street, Markham, Ontario, Canada L3R 1B4
Penguin Books (NZ) Ltd, 182–190 Wairau Road, Auckland 10, New Zealand

Penguin Books Ltd, Registered Offices: Harmondsworth, Middlesex, England

First published 1989
10 9 8 7 6 5 4 3 2 1

Typeset in Linotron Times by
Rowland Phototypesetting (London) Ltd
Printed in Great Britain by
Butler and Tanner Ltd, Frome and London

A CIP catalogue record for this book is available from the British Library
ISBN 0–670–82728–2

Contents

Willie Goes Exploring

Mum and Dad and Jenny and Henry lived at 3, Orange-blossom Avenue. Henry was eight and had a pet mouse. It lived in a cage in his bedroom. Jenny was five. She didn't have a pet mouse but she would have liked one.

Willie Whiskers lived at 3, Orangeblossom Avenue. His front door was a little hole in the skirting board of the kitchen. His back door led to the larder. This was the most important part of the house for Willie Whiskers and his family. It was full of good things to eat.

Willie Whiskers lived with his mum and dad, Mr and Mrs Whiskers, and all his brothers and sisters. There were lots of brothers and sisters. Willie Whiskers wasn't sure how many. Some days he thought there were nine and some days he thought there were ten.

Willie Whiskers couldn't

count very well. He was also
bad at adding up. He was best
at eating up. He was fat. He
was very fat. He looked like a
hairy golf ball.

"A young mouse should not
be so round," said Mr
Whiskers.

"What?" said Willie

Whiskers. He was dreaming of biscuit crumbs.

"You're too fat," said Mrs Whiskers. "If you're not careful, you'll get stuck one day."

Every morning the little mice had lessons. One day, Mr Whiskers decided to teach them how to add up.

"Now, sit down all of you

and we'll do some addition,"
he said.

"What?" said Willie
Whiskers. He was dreaming of
spilt ice-cream.

"Adding up," said Mrs Whiskers.

They all sat down like good little mice and did their sums. All, that is, except Willie Whiskers. Pictures started to float through his mind. 2 gingernuts + 3 chocolate biscuits + 7 chocolate-chip cookies... Willie felt quite faint. "I must be empty," he thought.

He put down his paper and pencil, and slipped away through the back door and along a short passage to the larder. Mr and Mrs Whiskers had made a tiny hole that led into the larder. Willie Whiskers rarely used this hole. It took so long when all his family was there. It didn't seem sensible to

be queuing when he could be
eating. Willie had made his own
little hole. No one else knew
about it. It was round the back

and up the side, and came out
on the top shelf.

The top shelf was the biscuit
shelf. Willie Whiskers

spent many happy after-
noons up there among the
cream crackers and the

chocolate fingers, when he should have been doing his lessons.

Today his shelf was full. "Someone's been shopping," he said.

"I'll have a nibble of this," he said to a packet of custard creams. "I'll have a bite of this," he said to a box of shortbread.

Willie Whiskers felt better. "I'll just have a look at the lower shelves," he decided.

He missed his footing and bounced right down to the bottom shelf, where there were

dark-green, cobwebby bottles.
They had labels that said things
like gin and whisky and brandy.

"Bother," he said. He was
too tired to climb up.

"Stale biscuits," he muttered.
He squeezed under the larder

One more try

door. No one was about. There
was a trail of toast crumbs
which Willie cleared up as he
went. The trail led into the

sitting-room, and was joined
by some biscuit crumbs that
were scattered all round Dad's
armchair. Willie Whiskers
tidied those up as well.

He suddenly felt very sleepy.
His eyes started to shut. He saw
a pair of slippers in the corner.

fluffy
lining

He crept into the left one. It was
soft and warm and fluffy. The
very thing. He went straight to
sleep.

Mum came home. Henry came home. Jenny came home. Mum put Dad's slippers to warm by the fire.

Dad came home. He was cross. He had had to wait ages for a bus. He saw the slippers and he felt better. He put on the right one. Lovely. He put on the left one. Struggle, push, struggle. He couldn't get his foot in.

Willie Whiskers dreamt that a hippopotamus was sitting on him. He was getting flatter and flatter and... He woke up. He sank his teeth into Dad's toe.

"OUCH!" exclaimed Dad.
He flung the slipper into the air
and hopped up and down on
one leg.

"Henry, if you let that mouse
out again," said Dad, "it's
going back to the pet shop."

"But, Dad..." said Henry.

24

Willie Whiskers tumbled out
of the slipper and made a dash
for the mousehole. He was so
flattened he got in quite easily.

"Where have you been?"
asked Mrs Whiskers.

"You haven't done your
addition," said Mr Whiskers.

"What?" said Willie.

"Adding up," said Mrs
Whiskers.

Willie Goes to School

Willie Whiskers and his nine, or
was it ten, brothers and sisters
were doing take away sums.
Willie tried hard, but a noise
somewhere between his toes
and his ears interrupted him. It

was that tummy of his. It was rumbling again.

"Mustn't let it disturb anyone," he thought. "Better top it up a bit."

He put down his paper and

pencil very quietly and crept
out into the passage. Once out
of sight, he scampered along to
his hole in the larder wall. He
climbed up and hopped in.

The larder looked a bit
empty. "Stale biscuits," he
muttered. "Someone needs to
do some shopping."

He took a rice-crispie and put
it back. He wanted something
more interesting. A little treat

to help him forget his take away sums. A breeze wafted past his nostrils. His nose twitched. His whiskers shook. There was a lovely smell. He had to follow it.

He climbed down to the shelf that was filled with the dark-green, cobwebby bottles. He squeezed under the larder door, ran across the kitchen and found himself in the hall. He followed his nose. He clambered over some shoes, and found a row of coats and hats and jackets all hanging up together. He sniffed Dad's jacket. Tobacco and beer. He sniffed Mum's coat. Mothballs. Just a minute; Henry's jacket.

"Here we are," thought Willie.

Willie Whiskers hopped into the first pocket. No. Second.

No. Third. Yes. There it was – a
half-eaten bar of chocolate with
a squidgy peppermint centre.
He didn't even have to open it.

"I'll have that," he said.

Some time later, Willie's
tummy rumble had quite
disappeared. So had the
chocolate. He settled down for
a little snooze under the bits of

string, chewing-gum wrappers
and crumpled tissues in the
corner of Henry's pocket. No
one would find him there. He

didn't really want to go home
until the take away sums were
over.

It was time for Henry to go to
school.

"Work hard," said Mum.

"Yes, Mum," said Henry.

"And don't take your mouse
to school," said Dad.

"No, Dad," said Henry.
He grabbed his jacket and
ran out of the house.

Willie Whiskers dreamt he was
in a big sailing ship. He sailed

into a storm. The wind blew
hard and the waves got bigger.
The boat was going up and
down, up and down.

After register, teacher showed
the children how to do take
away sums. Henry felt in his
pocket. He was sure he'd left
half a bar of chocolate there to
help him with his sums. All he

could find among the string, tissues and fluff was a minced-up wrapper. He didn't find the chocolate and he didn't find Willie.

Willie Whiskers slept on in Henry's untidy pocket. He dreamt that the storm was over and the ship had dropped anchor by an island covered in chocolate-bar trees. He swam ashore and ran across the warm

sand. He was just about to pick
a pawful of chocolate bars when
he woke up. He peeped out of
Henry's pocket.

"And then you carry one,"
said the teacher.

"Oh, horrors. Not take away
sums," thought Willie. "They
seem to be everywhere."

His nostrils twitched and his
whiskers trembled. A lovely
smell wafted past his nose. The

chocolate bar in his tummy had
sunk down. He was beginning
to feel empty again.

He crept out of Henry's
pocket and ran across lots of
pairs of knees. Some were
warm and some were cold.
Some were clean and some
were dirty.

"Miss!"

"Miss! There's a . . ."

"Miss!"

"Miss! I've just seen a . . ."

Willie Whiskers squeezed under the classroom door and scuttled along the corridor. He ran over the headmaster's shiny

shoes and round the secretary's high-heels, and all the time the wonderful smell grew stronger. It was an exciting mix of stew and custard and baked beans and treacle, mixed up with a few other things.

He stopped. He sniffed.

There it was – the school
kitchen. Big, big saucepans of

stew and cabbage and mashed
potato and rice pudding and
peas and prunes and carrots
and other treats. He tried to
keep calm. He'd never seen
so much food before. Why
bother with a larder? He'd
often heard Henry and Jenny

talk about school dinners.

"Yuk," said Henry.

"Yuk, yuk," said Jenny.

Willie didn't think it was yuk
at all. It was lovely.

"I'll have a bit of this," he
said to the stew, "and a bit of
that," he said to the rice

pudding. "And a mouthful of
these," he said to some bright-

green peas, "and a nibble of that," he said to an enormous pan of cauliflower cheese with crispy bits round the edge. When he was full up, he nestled down among a pile of warm oven gloves.

He woke with a jolt. The kitchen was full of people

clattering plates and spoons
and rushing around with trays
and pans.

Willie Whiskers was startled.
He climbed over a knobbly
trayful of hot sausages. He
tripped and landed on a
gigantic iced sponge and
skidded straight into an

enormous pan of warm, yellow
custard.

"Ooh, lovely," cried Willie
Whiskers.

A large lady with a large
ladle scooped him up with a
helping of custard, and plonked
him into a dish already
occupied by a piece of iced
sponge. She handed the dish to
a small boy wearing a familiar
jacket.

"Thanks," said Henry.
Henry walked slowly to his

table. His custard seemed
rather lively and his sponge
cake was swimming towards
him. It had two bright little eyes.

"A mouse," he whispered, "a
mouse in my custard." Henry

couldn't believe his luck. He
scooped Willie out and popped
him in his pocket.

Willie Whiskers cleaned his
fur. The custard was delicious.

"Very warm." He shut one
eye.

"Very comfortable." He
dozed off.

After school Henry went home.
He opened the front door. He
was going to sneeze. He
reached for his hanky and

pulled out Willie Whiskers
instead.

Henry sneezed.

"Ugh, uggh, ugggh," said
Willie. He ran as fast as he

could to his mousehole.

"Wherever have you been?" asked Mrs Whiskers.

"I suppose you got stuck somewhere," said Mr Whiskers. "You haven't done your subtraction."

"My what?" said Willie Whiskers.

"Taking away," said Mrs Whiskers.

Willie and the Birthday Cake

Willie Whiskers and his brothers and sisters were learning "How to Escape from Cats". Willie had to be the cat for this lesson. He liked

jumping out on his brothers and
sisters and giving them a fright,
but after a while he got bored.
While they were searching for
new hiding-places, he crept out

of the room, along the passage
and round to his hole in the
larder wall.

Inside, the larder looked
different. There were lots of
new, interesting-looking

packets on his biscuit shelf. He
climbed down a shelf.
Everything looked much
prettier than usual.

There was a stripy jelly,
plates of sandwiches, bowls of
crisps and peanuts. There were

little chocolate cakes, bigger
cherry cakes and one enormous
cake on a stand. It was so

beautiful, it took Willie Whiskers' breath away.

It had thick pink icing all over and a row of little white sugar flowers round the edge. There was a white satin ribbon tied round the side and six pink candles in the middle. Around the candles it said Happy Birthday Jenny in white icing.

Willie was overcome. He just stood quietly in the middle of all those lovely things and looked at them.

Then he said, "I'll have a bit of that," to a plate of cheese sandwiches. "I'll have some of

that," he said to the bowls of crisps and peanuts.

Then his throat felt a bit scratchy, so "I'll have a bite of that," he said to the plate of stripy jelly.

Willie Whiskers was beginning to get full, so he thought he'd miss out the chocolate and cherry cakes. He grasped the edge of the cake-stand, gave three big swings and was up beside the pink icing, the white ribbon and the sugar flowers.

He didn't know where to begin. He didn't want to spoil the cake.

"I'll just have that," he said to a sugar flower.

Pretty

He climbed up on to the top of the cake and sniffed at the

words Happy Birthday Jenny.

"Um, butter icing," sniffed Willie. "I'll just have a little bit." He ate the H from Happy.

"I'll just have a little bit more," he said, and ate the ny at the end of Jenny.

He meant to stop but it tasted

I wish I could spell

so good. Perhaps he'd better have some of the middle word just to even it up.

"That's enough," he said. He

didn't want to spoil the pattern.

Willie Whiskers was very full now. "I'll just put my feet up for a second," he murmured.

He burrowed into the side of the cake and curled up in the soft light sponge.

"I'll go home soon," he said,
and went to sleep.

"I don't want her to come to my
party," said Jenny.

"You must invite her. She's
your cousin," said Mum.
   Cousin Clarinda had blue

eyes and yellow curls and was good at lessons. She was terrified of mice.

Cousin Clarinda came to the party. She came in a blue, frilly

dress, which was the same colour as her eyes. She had lots of blue ribbons in her yellow hair. She looked lovely.

"Isn't she a picture?" said
Aunt Mavis.

"That dress matches her
eyes," said Aunt Matilda.

"And so well behaved," said
Aunt Muriel.

"I'm not going to like this
party," thought Jenny.

Henry offered to bring down

his pet mouse to give Cousin Clarinda a fright.

"If you do, you'll get no birthday cake," said Mum.

"If you do, that mouse goes straight back to the pet shop," said Dad.

So Henry didn't.

They played several games. Cousin Clarinda won all of

them. Then they went into the kitchen for tea. Mum hadn't brought the cake in yet. She was keeping it as a surprise. No one noticed the little nibbled bits in the sandwiches or the holes in the jelly. Everyone was getting full. Some of the naughtier girls were starting to flick peanuts at each other. Henry joined in. Clarinda didn't. Mum decided it was time to bring in the cake.

"Oh no!" said Mum.

"Oh no!" said Dad.

"Oh no!" said Jenny.

On top of the cake it said appy day Jen.

"I knew they couldn't spell at that shop," said Dad.

"Cut the cake, birthday girl," said Mum.

Jenny decided she must be nice to Cousin Clarinda. She cut

the first piece especially large and gave it to Clarinda.

Clarinda didn't have time to say thank you. A small, furry ball rolled out of the cake, off the plate, across the table and bounced into Clarinda's lap.

Clarinda gave a piercing shriek and fainted. Clarinda hit the floor.

Which way to the mousehole?

So did Willie Whiskers. He scampered across Clarinda's frilly blue skirts, got caught in her yellow hair, got tied up in her ribbons, and then made a dash for the mousehole.

"Where have you been?"
asked Mrs Whiskers.

"I'm not sure," said Willie.

Willie the Hero

Mum had gone to work. Henry had gone to school. Jenny had gone to school. Dad was in a hurry to get to work. He drank his tea and rinsed his cup. He grabbed his jacket and ran out to catch the bus. He had left the kitchen tap on.

Mrs Whiskers was giving everyone grooming lessons. How to arrange whiskers

neatly. How to wash properly behind the ears. How to keep a tail well scrubbed and neatly curled when not in use.

Willie Whiskers enjoyed
grooming lessons. Although he
knew he was a bit fat, he felt he
was a fine figure of a mouse. He

went to look at himself in the mirror by the back door. As he was so near the larder, he thought he might as well check the shelves.

There was a nice, moist, crumbly apple pie with just a slice missing. "I'll have some of this," he said.

There was a lump of cheese on a plate. "I'll have

a bit of that," he said.

He was beginning to get full.
He scuttled down to the
cobwebby shelf at the bottom of

the larder and rolled under the door.

Perhaps there was something nice to eat in the kitchen.

"Ah, the bread bin. Shut. Never mind." He squeezed his nose under the lid and levered it up. Wonderful. Brown bread, white bread and lots of convenient crumbs. "I'll tidy these up," he said.

He remembered Jenny's party. Surely there would be a few tasty bits and pieces on the floor? No. Someone had cleared up well. Anyway, the

floor looked funny. It was shiny. Wet. Yes, that was it. Wet. Very wet.

He heard a tinkly sound.
The tap was on. The sink was
full. Water was slopping

over the edge. Willie Whiskers
was full of apple pie, cheese and
breadcrumbs, but for once he
was wide awake. He slid down
the refrigerator flex and

part running, part swimming,
got to the mousehole just before
the water. His whiskers went in,

his nose went in and so did his ears and front paws, and then . . .

"I'm stuck," he said. "Help," he wailed, "I'm stuck."

Too much apple pie, too many breadcrumbs.

"Help," he yelled. "I can't come home." He started to cry.

Mum came running. "Why, Willie Whiskers," she said, "whatever is the matter? Why don't you stop crying and come right in?"

"Can't," sobbed Willie.

"Oh," said Mrs Whiskers, "I see. You're stuck!"

Mr Whiskers came running.

"If you can't come in, you'd better go out," he said.

Willie Whiskers did a little wriggle. Water started to slop in around him.

"Stop," said Mrs Whiskers. "What's happening?"

"There's a flood," said Willie. "That's why I came, I mean that's why I tried to come . . ."

He gave a little sob, "home."

"Stay there," said Mr
Whiskers.

"I'd rather not," said Willie.
"My bottom is cold and my tail
is freezing."

"Please," said Mrs Whiskers.

"Please," said all the nine,
or was it ten, brothers and
sisters. How could he say no?

Mrs Whiskers read him
stories about brave mice, and
Mr Whiskers tried again to
teach him take away sums,

although Willie would have preferred him not to. His brothers and sisters played sitting-still games with him like I Spy with my Little Eye, and

I Spy something beginning with W

combed his whiskers.

After a while, Willie
Whiskers noticed water oozing
in around him. He heard a

rumbling noise somewhere
around his middle.

"It's my tummy," he said,
"my tummy's going down. Fill
me up again or the water will
get in."

So all day Mr and Mrs
Whiskers and Willie's brothers

and sisters made a chain to
the larder and back. They

fed Willie with gingernuts and
apple pie and cheese. His

brothers and sisters moved so
quickly that Willie found
counting them even more

difficult than usual. He decided
there must be twelve of them.

Willie filled the hole
beautifully. No more drops of
water squeezed past his
middle.

"Willie Whiskers is a hero,"

said Mr Whiskers.

"Willie Whiskers is a hero,"
said Mrs Whiskers.

"Our Willie is a hero," said
all his brothers and sisters.

When Mum got back from
work, she waded into the
kitchen and turned off the tap.
It took a long time for the water

to go down. Just as the last of
the water drained away, and
Mum and Henry and Jenny and
Dad were mopping away in
their wellies, Jenny thought she
saw a small, brown, furry
bottom and little pink tail in the
skirting board. She watched it
give several wriggles and

disappear into a tiny hole in the
skirting.

For the rest of the day Willie was a hero. It felt very nice. No one did any lessons. They kept

saying "Thank you," and bringing even more apple pie and gingernuts. But for the first and probably the last time in his life, Willie Whiskers couldn't eat another crumb.

Mr Whiskers even brought

him a tot of whisky from one of the cobwebby bottles in the bottom of the larder. He said he had siphoned it off specially, to warm up Willie Whiskers' tail.

Willie took a sip. He felt as if he had drunk flames. His tail, which had been a bluish-purple, glowed pink. Mrs Whiskers rubbed his fur down and gave him two hot-water bottles.

"I'm a hero," said Willie Whiskers. "I'm a hero because I eat too much and because I'm so fat," said Willie. "I must get fatter," he said, and fell fast asleep.

The End